THE FELLOWSHIP OF AMOROUS GENTLEMEN

Borgo Press Books by Michael Hemmingson

Auto/Ethnographies: Sex, Death, and Symbolic Interaction
The Dirty Realism Duo: Charles Bukowski and Raymond Carver
The Fellowship of Amorous Gentlemen
How to Have an Affair and Other Instructions
In the Background Is a Walled City
Judas Payne
The Rose of Heaven
Sexy Strumpets and Troublesome Trollops
Seven Women: An Erotic Private Investigation
Star Trek: A Post-Structural Critique
The Stripper: A Tale of Lust and Crime
Zona Norte

FOR OTHER PRESSES

The Naughty Yard (Permeable Press, 1994)
Crack Hotel (Permeable Press, 1995)
Minstrels (Permeable Press, 1997)
The Mammoth Book of Short Erotic Novels (Carroll & Graf, 2000)
The Mammoth Book of Legal Thrillers (Carroll & Graf, 2001)
Wild Turkey (Forge, 2001)
The Comfort of Women (Blue Moon, 2002)
The Dress (Blue Moon, 2002)
My Fling with Betty Page (Eraserhead Press, 2003)
Drama (Blue Moon, 2003)
The Rooms (Blue Moon, 2003)
The Lawyer (Blue Moon, 2003)
House of Dreams Trilogy (Avalon, 2004)
The Garden of Love (Blue Moon, 2004)
Expelled from Eden: A William T. Vollmann Reader (Thunder's
    Mouth Press, 2004)
*This Other Eden (*The Dybbuk Press, 2009)
Amateurs (Olympia Press, 2009)
William T. Vollmann: A Critical Study (McFarland, 2009)
William T. Vollmann: An Annotated Bibliography (Scarecrow Press,
    2010)
Gordon Lish and His Influence on 20th Century American Literature
    (Routledge, 2010).
The Reflexive Gaze of Critifiction (Guide Dog Books, 2010)
Women in the Short Stories of Raymond Carver (McFarland, 2010)

Erotic Victorian Encounters with

THE
FELLOWSHIP OF
AMOROUS GENTLEMEN

*Based on the Memoirs of That Redoubtable
Explorer and Globe-Trotter, the Honorable*

PHILEAS FOGG, ESQ.

As Transcribed and Edited by

MICHAEL HEMMINGSON

THE BORGO PRESS

An Imprint of Wildside Press LLC

MMIX

CONTENTS

Publisher's Note 7

About Michael Hemmingson 8

Preface 9

A Young Wench's Log with Fog 17

A Vulgar Manuscript 87

Appendix: The Strange Case of C.'s Return 143

Dedicated to Mr. Jules Verne,
an extraordinary gentleman of fine letters.

I do miss him dearly.

PUBLISHER'S NOTE

The following comprises of a journal found among the possessions of an anonymous family estate and auctioned off at Sotheby's. Authentication was made. It was purchased by an unnamed party and handed over to The Borgo Press for publication. The materials, when gathered, appeared to have been in the process of being printed and bound by an unknown publisher in London, as evidence by the handwritten "Preface" of an editor known as Charles Kinbote. No historical records that we have checked uncover a "Charles Kinbote" working in the blossoming British publishing industry in the late 1800s; it could be this was a pen name for T. S. Elliot and that the firm he worked for had, in the end, declined to release this journal to the public for any number of social and legal ramifications.

The journal, composed by an unknown young lady of the Victorian era known only as "C." were written in large penmanship in small binder but in no discernable or logical order; indeed, at times some pages were indecipherable and some seem to be missing.

—R.R.

ABOUT MICHAEL HEMMINGSON

MICHAEL HEMMINGSON, an independent scholar, spends his time between Los Angeles and San Diego. His first feature film, *The Watermelon*, was released on DVD and Blu-Ray in 2009 from LightSong Films and Celebrity Video Distributors. He directed and narrated a short documentary, *Life in Zona Norte*, for Real Ideas Studio, which screened at the 2009 Cannes Film Festival. His critical studies include *The Dirty Realism Duo: Charles Bukowski and Raymond Carver* (2008); *William T. Vollmann* (2009); *The Role of Women in Raymond Carver's Short Fiction and Life* (2010); and *Gordon Lish and His Influence on 20th Century American Literature* (2010). He has also published some novels, short story collections, and edited a handful of anthologies, from *The Mammoth Book of Legal Thrillers* (2001) to *First Person Sociology* (2010).

PREFACE

I was there, that day, at the Reform Club, when Mr. Phileas Fogg won, in a game of cards (whist, to be exact) the sexual captivity of a one Mr. Henry Parker's mysterious niece: a beautiful young lady many of us had seen in the better parts of London, always on the arm of her dastardly uncle—indeed, a shy girl possessing curly, reddish-blonde hair and pale, lightly freckled skin and exquisite green eyes that made many unmarried men (and the married gents as well, it goes without saying) take a long glance and wonder.

This was in March of 1875; I am not certain of the exact date. I am afraid that I tend to be amiss in these small details, despite my profession as a man of the published letters.

The card game was not going in Henry Parker's favor, and he was known to be a man who did not like to lose (and had a bit of a temper).

Contrary, Mr. Phileas Fogg was a man known to hardly, if ever, lose at either of whist or wager. I knew for a fact this was something he greatly prided himself on.

There were half a dozen gentlemen, including yours truly, watching this game with what I would call snide English interest. Mr. Parker was tapped out of funds, every single pound note now in Mr. Fogg's possession.

'Shall we call it a day, sir?' said Fogg.

'I will win my money back and more, sirrah,' said Mr. Parker, barely keeping his anger inside that singular ruddy skin. 'My credit is good, we both bank at Baring's, so when I offer a cheque I trust you will honor it as good as money.'

Fogged leaned back in his chair and smiled. He stated, 'I have something else in mind, other than money, for you to wager, Mr. Parker.'

'And what would that be, Mr. Fogg?'

'Tell me first, are you a man of your absolute word?'

'When I say I will wager,' returned Parker, 'I mean it.'

'Very well,' said Mr. Fogg, 'wager your lovely niece. What is her name? C. Yes. She will do just fine.'

There was a mumbling among the men at the Club.

'Are you out of your mind, Mr. Fogg?' cried Henry Parker.

'Not in the least, sir,' said Phileas Fogg. 'It is no secret—as few scandals *are* secret—that you have your niece enslaved to your puerile favor. What you have over her head I can only speculate, and is none of my business. I would, however, enjoy engaging in a certain *business* with the girl.'

'Are you insinuating my niece is a whore?' said Mr. Parker, nearly rising out of his large chair.

'What would you call her then?' asked Mr. Fogg, raising a brow and scratching his beard.

Parker sat down and let out a heavy sigh. He nodded. 'A trollop,' he conceded, 'a dirty strumpet, that girl.'

'Enticing.'

'I do not know what kind of man you honestly believe me to be, a devil or a lout,' said Henry Parker, 'but I will not gamble the body of my own favorite niece.'

'Then you must be uncertain of your hand, and your ability to win—nay, to win against me, a man who never loses at a game of cards.'

'Oh, Mr. Fogg, I assure you of my certainty, but I do not make it a habit of wagering the pleasures of young women like some sort of vile flesh merchant out of the Ottoman Empire.'

There was a moment of silence while the two men stared at and considered one another.

'Since our mutual credit is in good standing,' said Mr. Fogg, 'I shall then propose to raise the stakes to ten thousand pounds.'

'Ten thousand!' said Mr. Parker, his face going the way of the colour red.

'Can you meet this amount? Or can you not?' asked Fogg.

'Indeed I *can.*'

'And so?'

'So be it,' said Henry Parker, who immediately lost the game to the predictable and smug Mr. Fogg. Parker was a rapidly humble man, and he said to Fogg: 'I beseech you, sirrah, such an amount will financially crush me.'

'What are you telling me, my dear friend?' asked a rather amused Fogg.

'I propose we return to your previous suggestion,' said Parker. 'The question of C.'s ownership.'

'Yes,' said Fogg, smiling and sitting back in his large chair and stroking his moustache in an agreeable manner, 'we can do that. She is an exquisite example of the opposite sex, whore or not.'

'And I assume you will take possession of the girl for the rest of her life? Or—'

'Mr. Parker! I am a man who owns no slaves. C. will come and live at my home and do for me what she has been doing for you...let us say, for a period of eighty days.'

'Eighty days!' said Parker, and with some amusement he added: 'A number you are now famous for.'

There was constrained laughter in the room.

'What can I say?' returned Fogg. 'I have always been a man of impeccable consistency.'

'I shall deliver her to you this evening,' Henry Parker promised.

* * * * * *

As far as I, or anyone else, knew, Henry Parker made good on his word. Neither he nor Phileas Fogg ever discussed the matter further at the Reform Club, but from that day on Parker was never seen in London with his niece by his side; the lass, in fact, was never seen again. Oh, there were rumors, and I listened to this scuttlebutt with great interest. Strange and sordid tales of wanton debauchery between Fogg and the girl, as well as her being given to such great men as Captain

Nemo and a certain amateur detective (who must remained unnamed) for a night of perversion and abandon. Did I believe such tales? I knew very well how gossip could be stretched like a tortured body (in one of de Sade's dungeons, no less) from the actual truth.

Nevertheless, this was all sweet candy for the lascivious imagination!

In early 1878 I was employed as a book editor and while some of the novels I acquired for my company were of the highest caliber of literature, others were nothing more than pure filth—the kind of material that helps keep a publisher within the margin of profit. One day, while at the Reform Club, the matter of Phileas Fogg and C. Parker came up in conversation—oh, the many speculations of what might have transpired in bed between the two were whispered and chattered (and laughed) about at great length!

One man said: 'I understand she kept a journal of her eighty days with grand old Phileas.'

'If such a thing exits,' said I, although I did not think it did, 'I would publish it at my firm, sight unseen.'

'That could be arranged,' another man said.

'Oh?'

'If you are willing to pay good money.'

'If this log is real, yes indeed. But I have my doubts.'

'I will contact you within the week, Mr. Kinbote.'

* * * * * *

Eight days later, I found myself waiting—on a rainy, foggy day—in a dimly lit cobblestone London alley. It was a cold evening and I was about ready to leave, believing this foolish and thinking myself an imbecile to take these asinine measures. It was then that a short, wobbling man donning a bowler's hat appeared.

'Mr. Kinbote?' He had a French accent.

'Yes.'

'My name is Jean Passepartout. Manservant to Mr. Phileas Fogg.'

'Of course. I have seen you with him before.'

The little man, who had very sad eyes, removed a leather-bound journal from inside his thick coat. 'This is the log, as transcribed by Mademoiselle Parker. It is, I must warn you, what we French call "a dirty book."'

I said, 'I hope so.'

'Did you bring the money?'

I handed him an envelope stuffed with bank notes.

'The lady has one request before we make this transaction,' he said. 'That if you publish this, it is to be anonymous. Her actual name shall never appear on the book.'

'To that,' said I, 'you and the woman have my word.'

After all, how would I publish it otherwise?

He took the envelope and I possessed the memoir, the contents* of which you, Dear Reader, now hold in your trembling (with desirous) hands.

Read this account at your own risk, to either the betterment or detriment of your heart, mind, body, and soul.

—Charles Kinbote
London
20 October 1879

---

* But it goes without saying that a published version of this journal has never seen print until this day in the Year of Our Lord MMIX. –M.H.

A YOUNG WENCH'S
LOG WITH FOGG

INSTALLMENT I: *In which I learn of my Uncle's wager and loss as well as an account of what happened the first night at Mr. Fogg's estate.*

At the request of my present master and owner, Mr. Phileas Fogg of much renowned adventures (or so I have been told and led to believe, but one can never truly trust the words that come out of the mouths of such devious men), I am keeping this journal of my days under his submission and whim. To begin, how did I get here? My story would have to start with my father's untimely death due to the pneumonia and, six months later, my mother's subsequent demise due to a broken heart, and the many debts that my father left which were passed on to her, and then to me and my younger brother. Things appeared dire in those dark days, but my dear Uncle Henry made a trip from London to Essex and assured me that he would take care of certain affairs and amounts outstanding, and all would then be fine. He kissed my hand, and then kissed my cheek, and then tried to kiss me on the mouth. I would not let him kiss me on the mouth! I recognized the way he looked at me, I had seen men stare at me in such a fashion—usually elderly gents with bad intentions. Uncle Henry's intentions were just as base for on that first night he came into my bedchamber and forced himself upon me. I knew it was wrong but deep down I, for some unfathomable reason, enjoyed what happened more than I wish to confess. Perhaps this had to do with some of the fantasies and dreams I had at night about marauding pirates and Vikings. I did not, however, let my Uncle know of my secret pleasure; instead, I wept like a fragile creature and cried, 'How could you do this to me? I am seventeen and *was* a virgin. What man will marry me now?'

'I shall marry you,' he said, 'it is the only just thing to do.'

'But that is not possible, Uncle Henry!'

'I have had you once, girl, and I fear I will not be able to stop myself and have to have you again and again. So I should make you my wife, although I know very well the law will not allow such a union.'

'Then have me!' I said, not quite the chaste young lady any longer; and after he made love to me a second time, he understood that I enjoyed the sin we were committing.

'You are nothing but a whore,' he said, and again I wept. 'I have a proposition for a whore such as yourself,' said he, 'I have cleared all your father's unfortunate debts and I shall enroll your brother to finest boarding school where he will learn to be a gentlemen of the world, and you shall come and live with me, and share my bed whenever I desire...and I have *great* desire, that I can assure you.'

Yes, Dear Reader, I am but a *whore*, a girl who enjoys every manner of illicit intercourse. Damn the Bible and all its restrictions! I have never been a religious girl. By agreeing to my Uncle Henry's terms, I essentially became his sex slave. I even signed a contract to such, binding me to his loins and releasing me at the age of twenty-five.

As I write in this log, I am nineteen, and my uncle has given me to Mr. Phileas Fogg for sexual pleasure.

Imagine my dismay when Uncle Henry told me what happened! He had lost a bet, he said, and I was the goods he no longer owned.

I was shocked, yes, but I was not surprised.

'Oh, Uncle,' said I, 'how could you?'

'It is only for eighty days,' said he.

'But I do not know this man!' said I.

'And have you not, for my visual enjoyment, coupled with gentlemen you did not know?' asked my Uncle.

He had a point but I told him I did not want to do this.

'You have no choice,' he reminded me, 'for we have a contract, and the contract says you shall always be submissive to me, and do anything and everything I say.'

I packed some clothing and was dispatched by carriage to No. 7, Saville Row, Burlington Gardens. The property was a handsome estate, much more refined and civil-looking than my Uncle's. Mr. Phileas Fogg, whom I only knew by reputation, turned out to be a handsome man himself, much to my relief, and not much older than my Uncle (his mid-forties, I would say). Fogg resembled a bearded, tranquil Byron—well, this is what Mr. Fogg has instructed me to write in these pages.

'Am I not Byronic?' was the first thing he said to me.

'Yes, sir,' I said, meekly.

'And you, young lady, are enjoyable to the eye.'

'Thank you.'

'I am impatient to see you completely naked,' he said. 'Oh, we will have grand times together!'

'I will do whatever you ask,' I said, so he would know that I was living up to whatever matters my Uncle had promised him.

Mr. Fogg showed me upstairs to what he said would be my bedchambers for the next eighty days. I was impressed by the size of the room, three times the size of what my Uncle was providing me, as well as the large canopied bed and the antique furniture that Mr. Fogg informed me were fifteenth-century Prussian.

'You are very kind,' I said; 'I hope I will be able to give you much pleasure during my stay.'

'It would please me, at this moment,' he said, 'to gaze upon your naked flesh.'

I removed my garments in the manner that my Uncle instructed, the way he said men liked to observe wanton women such as myself disrobe. Not the way a wife might do for a husband, no; but a way a whore does for a man she is about to fornicate with for money. Already I was wet between the legs by the very thought of this, and the excitement of the new situation I found myself in, caused goose bumps on my skin. Mr. Fogg sat on the bed and kept his eyes focused on my breasts and between my legs. He nodded with what looked like approval, uttering 'yes' and 'good' and smiling at me. 'Turn around,' said he, 'let me get a good look at your arse.' I did as I was told. 'Now spread the cheeks of your arse for me,' said he.

'But Mr. Fogg!' I protested, blushing.

'Are you or are you not my slave, young lady?' he queried of me.

'Yes, Mr. Fogg,' said I, 'you won me in your wager with my horrid Uncle, and I will do as you ask,' and so I did the naughty thing he asked and I liked it.

'You are a very bad girl,' Mr. Fogg stated.

'Yes,' I replied, 'I am.'

'It has occurred to me that you may require a spanking,' he said.

'This may be so.'

'Did Henry bend you over his knee?'

'In more than one way, sir.'

'Then I shall lay you across my lap, right here,' said Mr. Fogg, 'and make your tender arse a tad red.'

I understood what I had to do. I presented my bottom to him, lying across his legs. He slapped each cheek gently. 'Bad, bad girl,' he said with absolute delight.

I told him: 'You can hit me harder if you like.'

'How hard, my dear?'

'As hard as Mr. Fogg wishes.'

'It is not my wish to cause you pain.'

'Perhaps the desire for a little pain is *my* wish.'

'Oh, indeed, you are a bad girl!'

'Indeed.'

He spanked me harder.

'Do you like that, young strumpet?' he asked.

'Very much so, Mr. Fogg,' I returned.

'Shall I hit you harder?'

'If it pleases you, it pleases me.'

Back and forth, slap, slap, spank, spank, and then Mr. Fogg said, 'It would please me to feel how damp your cunny is,' and he inserted two fingers into my hole. My body quickly became spasmodic; I almost fell onto the floor.

'Mr. Fogg,' said I, 'it would please me to pleasure you with my mouth.'

'Oh,' he said, 'that would be most kind on your part.'

My knees were on the floor and my face was in his lap. I unbuttoned his trousers, perhaps too eagerly, and was surprised at the size of Mr. Fogg's lobcock: it was three times the size of my Uncle's.

So long and so thick, pulsing with monstrous veins and smelling like a chamber pot! I was not sure I could get my mouth around the head but I managed. I used two hands at the base of it and was fearful of the amount of man seed the giant member might shoot out. But Mr. Fogg said, 'I want to be inside you.' He said, 'I want to fuck you.' I had never heard that word used in such a manner, but I was well aware I was not here to get married, to be made love to; I was here to be fucked.

It was not easy for Mr. Fogg to slip it in, because of his girth. It was painful like the first time but after relaxing a great deal, my vagina stretched enough for him to fuck me. And he fucked me twice. And I enjoyed it very much.

'Will you stay with me?' I asked my new master. 'Or do you wish me to sleep in your bed?'

'I do not stay a full night with whores,' Mr. Fogg said, pulling up his trousers. 'Clean up, get a good night's rest, and I shall see you in the morning.'

He left me there with his man seed leaking from my madge and onto the bed; I felt split open and dirty, just the way I was supposed to feel, I surmise.

INSTALLMENT II: *In which I encounter Mr. Fogg's curious French manservant.*

Not fifteen minutes had passed when the door to my room opened. I expected Mr. Fogg and was happy that he wanted me again. Instead, a little man in servant's clothing came inside, carrying a tray with warmed milk and some biscuits. I quickly covered myself with the bedding. 'My name is Jean Passepartout, in the employ of Mr. Fogg,' said he. 'Do not be afraid, mademoiselle. Would you care for some warm milk?'

'Thank you,' I said, taking the milk and drinking it.

He watched me like one would look at a painting. 'You have an exquisite neck,' he said.

'Thank you, sir.'

'Now that you have that milk in your belly, would you like to drink the warm milk from my penis?'

'Sir,' said I, 'did Mr. Fogg send you in here for that?'

'He doe snot know I am here. In fact, he went out for a while, as he often does. I am here on my own accord, and I would like to sample the slut we will have under this roof for the next eighty days.'

'I do not make it a habit of putting strange little Frenchmen in my mouth!' I said.

'Then I will have the filth between your legs!' he yelled, jumping on top of me and holding my arms pinned above my head. 'You smell so disgusting!' he cried. *'C'est très magnifique!"*

'I've not cleaned myself,' I told him, 'since our master's visit.'

'It is my lot to clean up after my master,' said he, 'I do not mind wallowing in his scum!'

Passepartout's phallus was a small one, smaller than my Uncle's, and after the stretching I took from Mr. Fogg, I must admit I hardly felt the little man inside me. This did not seem to trouble the Frenchman, and he was done within a minute.

'Please excuse my outburst of lust,' he said, bowed, and left me there in the bed.

I ate the biscuits, drew a bath, and then went to sleep.

That is all, for now.

INSTALLMENT III: *In which my Master, Mr. Phileas Fogg, spanks my tender little arse again for being such a strumpet.*

It was before noon that my Master, Mr. Fogg, came to this room that is my prison. He sighed, stood above me and shook his head. I knew that something was wrong and that the end result was going to be pain and humiliation…I anticipated this greatly and felt myself getting wet between the legs.

'You wanton whore!' said he.

'Yes,' I said, for how could I deny such an accusation?

He then did what I expected, what I hoped for in my heart but would never admit with the words that come out of my dirty mouth: Mr. Fogg laid me across his lap and gave each of my cheeks a good spanking, stopping now and then to insert a finger into either of my two throbbing holes.

'It excites me,' said this gentleman who won me in a card game, 'to think of you being with another man like that. That gives me ideas, you see. I thought I would keep you all to myself, but I realize now that I must share my prize....'

'Send your manservant in then,' I told him in a haughty, maybe too defiant voice, 'send him in to do what he wants, and watch, because I have a feeling that watching is something you like to do.'

'Yes,' said Mr. Fogg, 'but right now....'

Right now he wanted me to get on my knees and take him in his mouth again. This is I did, yes I did; I would suck on his man root all day long if he required me.

When he was done and had greedily spent himself into my mouth, Mr. Fogg said, 'It is not Passepartout that I wish to see you with; in fact, that would be the antithesis of my desire. No; but there are others....'

'Others?' said I.

'Others,' said Mr. Fogg, 'whom I call my contemporaries, my colleagues, my friends. Extraordinary gentlemen—each and every one of them. Fascinating, secretive, and always up for fucking a pretty young lady such as yourself,' and with that, he stroked my face oh so very gently, and the quickly slapped it. He slapped me so hard that my brain rattled and I saw spots before my eyes. 'What do you have to say about that, wench?' he asked.

'I will do whatever you want,' I said.

'Of course you will.'

'I am yours.'

'I own your body, for the time being,' he said.

'Yes, Mr. Fogg, you do.'

'Don't forget it.'

'How could I?'

He slapped me again.

'And do not take that tone with me,' said he.

I nodded.

'Now,' he said, 'get on that bed so I can stick myself inside your body.'

INSTALLMENT IV: *In which my master, Mr. Ph** *

INSTALLMENT V: *In which I timidly ask Mr. Fogg about his alleged adventures.*

After he had his way with me, I lay in my new master's arms and he stroked my hair. For a moment, I almost felt as if we were a couple in love, or man and wife. I had a fantasy of him kissing me, and just when I was enraptured with the images in my head, and just when I was about to reach up and kiss the bearded man myself, he smacked my bottom good (as if he knew what I was thinking) and told me what a bad little girl I was.

This I knew, this I agreed. To this, I said, 'Yes, Mr. Fogg.'

And he hit my bottom again, but good, and I shuddered with delight at his burning and sturdy touch.

'Never in all my travels have I encountered such a wanton whore as yourself,' he said to me, softly, his lips close to my ear.

'Oh, Mr. Fogg,' said I, 'I do not believe you!'

'You doubt my word, wench?'

'I do, sir.'

He gave me a light smack for that.

'You should never doubt me,' said he, 'you should never doubt. Always keep that in mind, C.'

'Surely,' I said, 'you have met a lass or two much more horrible than I.'

'Perhaps,' he said, and as he spoke he nodded a little and stroked his fine blonde beard, 'but none so young. More often than not, it takes many years for a woman to reach such depths of depravity and continue to hold her composure such as you. To the age of twenty-seven or even thirty, based on my experience.'

'That is so old!' said I, but I was trying to be amusing.

Mr. Fogg laughed, but he had a serious look in his eyes. 'That is not, in the grand cosmic scale of all matters, not so old.'

'I suppose you are correct. I, however, shall never live to such an age, I fear.'

'And why do you say that, sweet little one?'

'It is something I simply know,' I told him, and I was quite serious about this.

'Is it that you do not wish to grow older,' he said, 'or do you feel that an unfortunate fate awaits you?'

'A little of both, it seems.'

'How so?'

'I am uncertain....'

'Tell me more.'

'I do not know if there is more to tell.'

He asked, 'Would you call it intuition? Have you had dreams? Visions? Have voices unknown to you spoken and said certain things?'

'I simply cannot see myself alive past the page of twenty,' I said.

'So soon!' he said.

'Maybe twenty-two, but no later,' I said. 'It all seems to far, far away. As if another life awaits me. And do I even want that life? Do I even want the life I have now.'

He laughed.

'You are amused,' I said, weakly. 'Mr. Fogg.'

'Yes,' he said, touching my hair and then my face, 'and a wee bit sad.'

'Sad?'

'To hear such words come out of such a pretty mouth.'

'My mouth is pretty,' I said in my best devious voice, 'when you place your whorepipe inside of it.'

'Your face is pretty too,' he said, 'as are your eyes, and your hair, and your arms, and your back, and your stomach, and your legs. That is, your entire body; your entire self; your entire being.'

'What of my soul?' asked I.

'I do not, yet, know your soul,' he said.

'And you do not want to,' I told him, 'for it is a wretched, ugly thing.'

'But not your body,' he said.

'This body is yours, Mr. Fogg,' I said.

'Indeed,' said he, and he mounted me rather quickly and this time the act of fucking was long and drawn out. We both sweated and made passionate sounds. I felt satisfied. I felt good.

We lay there next to each other again the way normal lovers should.

'Tell me about your adventures around the world, Mr. Fogg,' I suggested.

'What is there to tell?'

'I am certain you have much to say, sir.'

'And why do you think that?'

'I have heard—'

'Heard what, my wench?'

'Certain things.'

'Consisting of?'

'Your adventures,' said I. 'Nothing too specific. This and that. Things that seem impossible.'

'Impossible or implausible?'

'I do not know, sir.'

He sighed and said to me, 'There are so many stories, so many adventures, so much fact and so much that has been changed into fiction. I would not know where to begin.'

'So it's all true?' I asked.

'You doubt me?'

'Not at all.'

'What did I say…?'

'Never doubt you,' I said, 'and this, Mr. Fogg, I never shall.'

'Good, good,' said he, touching my hair and tangling it between his long fingers.

'So why are you not presently on an adventure now, Mr. Fogg?' I asked him a little later into the night.

'A hero cannot be out in the world non-stop,' he told me; 'all men of action must stop, relax, rest, and love.'

'What are you doing now, Mr. Fogg?'

'I am here in London,' he said, 'I am here with you, in Burlington Garden.'

INSTALLMENT VI: *In which Mr. Fogg brings me a gift.*

Today, my new master presented me with a book, wrapped in a silk cloth that he told me contained his dried semen. Not only was I surprised by the gesture, I was somewhat shocked by the title of the book, *The Dictionary of the Vulgar Tongue*, complied by Captain Francis Grose, *et al.*[*]

---

[*] Originally printed in 1785 and revised in 1811, it was a lexicon balatronicum; a dictionary of buckish slang, university wit, and pickpocket eloquence (and now considerably altered and enlarged, with the modern changes and improvements, by a member of the whip club.) Grose and his assistant Tom Cocking took midnight walks through London, picking up slang words in slums, drinking dens and dockyards and adding them into their 'knowledge-box'. *The Vulgar Tongue* was recognised throughout the 19th century as one of the most important collections of slang words in the English language, and it would strongly influence later dictionaries of slang. Grose, born in 1730, liked to eat rich foods and to drink port. He also liked to tell stories. A very fat man, he took pleasure in the pun linking his name to his size. He had a classical education before going on to study drawing. He was a member of the Society of Antiquaries and was made a captain in the Surrey Militia in 1778. It is surmised that the phrase "that's gross" may have been derived from the man's last name and his connection too all things untidy. –M.H.

Upon receiving this gift, I said, 'Oh.' I said, 'Oh my.'

'I believe you will find it amusing and useful,' said Mr. Fogg, and then he left the room and did not return for my favors that night. Nor did his manservant. I was alone with the book; I found the situation rather curious.

INSTALLMENT VII: *In which my master brings me the first man of renown, purely for his visual pleasure.*

Mr. Fogg came into my room tonight as I was hoping he would, for I found that I was beginning to miss his company. He was not alone; no, for standing next to him was another a man, a man taller and more statuesque than my master. This man had a dark, smooth complexion and the most piercing green eyes I had ever seen on any human being (I almost didn't believe they were real and had been craftily placed there by a doctor with good hands) (I guess I should make mention that those green eyes took in my entire body with one long glance going from my head to my toes). He wore a strange white hat, unlike any other hat I had ever seen; he wore a dark blue suit that seemed to be like a uniform, but it was unlike any other uniform I had ever seen; he wore knee-high black leather boots (the sight of them made my back tingle!) and a sword on his belt.

'Whore,' said Mr. Fogg, 'allow me to introduce to you a very important, very famous colleague—and friend—of mine, Captain Nemo.'

The exquisite man bowed and smiled.

'A captain!' said I.

'Indeed he is,' said Fogg.

'Of a ship?' I asked.

Both men looked at one another and then they laughed, deeply.

'Yes, a ship,' said Captain Nemo, 'you can say that the *Nautilus* is a ship.'

'A very special, and a very unique one,' concurred Mr. Fogg. 'But enough of this useless banter. Captain Nemo, I present to you C. The very girl I discussed with you last night.'

'Far more beautiful than you described, Phileas.'

I believe I may have blushed at that moment.

'Yes, well, I never have been the one with the proper words, now have I?'

'I shall have fun with this one, Phileas.'

'I know how you love to defile your women, Nemo, you old sea fearing scoundrel!'

I looked at my master with confusion.

'Don't give me those big, doe-like eyes, my dear,' Fogg said to me, 'you know very well why I have brought him to your chamber.'

I looked down.

'Eyes up!'

I looked up.

'So pretty,' said Captain Nemo, 'and yet so horrible.'

Again, the tingles in my back....

'Horrible?' said Fogg.

'That such beauty in the world exists, to be used so dastardly by wicked men such as ourselves,' stated Nemo.

To which Mr. Fogg replied: 'But is it not the right of men such as ourselves to do as we please, when we please, and as we see fitting? Yes?'

'Yes.'

'*I* am pleased that you agree.'

'I would, if you *please*, like to see this young harlot *naked,*' Nemo requested.

'Then it is done, as the day she was born,' returned Mr. Fogg, and to me: 'Disrobe at once. Show my compatriot here your body, you...you....'

My master did not know what naughty name to call me!

I nodded and did as I was told; I disrobed (which was easy, for I was only wearing a one piece of long bed clothing) and stood before both of them naked.

Naked.

And it felt good.

But I didn't let it show.

I blushed; I knew they would like this; I acted timid as my role as sex slave required. I covered my pubis with my clasped hands and when my master told me to take my hands away, I did.

'Ah yes,' said Nemo with approval in his deep and mysterious voice, as if that voice had come from the depths of many leagues under the sea, 'exquisite.' Then he came to me, slowly, and then fast, taking me in his mighty arms, smelling the skin at my neck and grabbing my buttocks.

'I hope you enjoy, old friend,' said Fogg.

'And what will you do?'

'I shall leave you be.'

'Is that what you really want?'

'Well....'

'What do you want, Phileas?'

'To watch.'

'Of course.'

'If you don't mind.'

'You always liked to watch, Phileas,' said Nemo, 'and I never minded before. Do as you will.'

'I shall sit here in this corner,' said my master, sitting in a chair, 'and I shall be quiet as a burglar in the night, as you do what you sailors do to poor innocent little girls.'

'Um, yes,' said Nemo, his hands all over my body now as he laid me on the bed, 'and what I think I shall do is bugger her arse.'

I made a sound, a sigh, quite audible—this was, of course, for effect and theatrics only.

'Wench,' Fogg told me, 'you will give this man what he requires. Do you understand?'

I nodded.

'Bugger her all you want,' Fogg said to Nemo, 'bugger the bitch until she is a puddle a trollop juice.'

Nemo took his time undressing; he never once took a break from his intense, lustful stare upon my body (most notably my buttocks) and I, in earnest return, also gazed upon his remarkable form.

And how remarkable it was! Just as I knew it would be. Oh, I had, by then, become a good judge of what a man would look like without his outer garments. I knew from the very first moment that Captain Nemo would be a beautiful naked man. His entire body was smooth, dark and virtually hairless, taut and chiseled with muscles in a most classical, Statue of David manner. His penis was thin but quite long; I shuddered at the notion that this would go into my arse at that full length. But did I really have either a say or choice in the matter?

The astute reader of this journal that I am keeping, whoever you may be (either man, woman or even child) knows what happened next. I said that Nemo's penis was lengthy so imagine how that must have felt all the way inside my innards! Did I enjoy the penetration? Being of the sluttish nature, I suppose that I did. Being but a girl with limited experience in the nature of being buggered, I could not help but scream.

I screamed, yes, lying there on the bed on my belly, Nemo behind me. Nemo leaned over and whispered in my ear and told me, 'Relax, my dear, and enjoy it.'

I looked at Mr. Fogg, across the room, watching; he appeared smug and pleased. I had seen the same visage upon my uncle after he had buggered me in past times.

My uncle never buggered me often, he said the mess disgusted him; but sometimes he would have too much to drink and get into one of his nasty, rough moods.

Nemo did not seem to mind the mess as he continued to slide his long member in and out of my arse for what seemed like an entire hour. I know I was making a mess because I could both feel it coming out of me and smell it. The undeniable aroma filled the room.

'So beautiful, so wonderful,' said Nemo under his heavy, foreign breath, 'so tight, so dirty...'

I wasn't sure how much more I could take; there was the agony but also the ecstasy of this horrid act was causing my body to be limp. Nemo pulled himself out of me and said, 'Come now, my dear, suck me clean.'

He placed the messy cock in front of my face. I think I may have flinched.

'Open your mouth, now, my dear,' Nemo said, sternly, 'it's not so bad, believe me.'

'Do as he says,' Fogg commanded me.

I closed my eyes, opened my mouth, and took Nemo's dirty log down my throat. I kept in mind that it was only myself. It was not, in fact, so bad; there was very little taste. After five or ten minutes, Nemo's manhood was clean as a whistle, as they say, and after another five minutes he shot his cannon off and his seed flowed down into my belly.

'Oh yes,' said Nemo, grabbing my head.

Only a sailor!

INSTALLMENT VIII: *In which my Master brings me the elderly great white hunter for a fuck.*

It was a week later when Mr. Fogg brought another one of his apparent 'famous' colleagues into my room to delight my nimble but usable body. This gentleman was elderly, thin, white-bearded, and dressed all in khaki and boots as if he were ready to go on safari.

Little did I know how correct my observations were!

'My eyes like what they see,' said the old gentleman.

'My dear C,' said Fogg, 'allow me to introduce you to the one and only Allan Quartermain.'

'Oh!' said I, 'oh my!' and I think I may have bowed; for indeed, I knew of this man's name, I had heard of and even read about his remarkable, if not questionable, adventures in Africa.

'The child knows who I am,' beamed Mr. Quatermain.

'And who does not, sir?' said Fogg.

'I didn't even know you were still alive!' I blurted like a fool.

Mr. Quatermain laughed loudly, but then he stopped and coughed.

'Easy there, old chap,' Fogg advised him, 'don't wear yourself before you've had your fun.'

'Nonsense!' retorted the great white hunter; 'I could take on and please half a dozen such comely lasses as she...*and still* do battle with a rhino!'

'Indeed, I believe you could.'

'Phileas, do not mock me.'

'Would I dare?'

'You have before.'

'Look at her,' Fogg said as he pointed at me, 'have her. *You,*' he told me, 'get naked *now!*'

I did as commanded by my owner.

'Oh well now isn't this splendid!' cried Quatermain as he pinched one of my nipples (quite hard!). He cleared his throat and turned his head. 'Phileas, are you just going to stand there?'

'I thought I might sit.'

'Oh, Phileas, please.'

'Right you are, old chap, old bean, old chum-bucket,' and with that, Mr. Fogg gave us a wink and left the room.

Quartermain sighed and shook his head. 'Phileas should know better,' he told me, pinching my other nipple, 'I have never engaged much in deviance, despite all my worldly travels.'

This was true; there is nothing extraordinary or odd to report in these pages about the coitus that ensued. It was by the book. I must, say, however, that I have never gone to a bed with a man of his advanced years and I felt very queer about the whole matter, like it was not natural. Mr. Quarter-main was, after all, somewhere in his seventies; yet despite his years, his cock was hard and worked well. But I did not find his body at all alluring—it was pasty white, marked with many scars, sagging flesh on his old bones really. His penis was average and he didn't have intercourse with me for too long of a time, and I was a bit fearful for his health al-though he seemed fit enough.

After, he asked me if I really, truly had heard of his name, or had Mr. Fogg told me to say that.

'I know who you are,' I said, 'and of some of your grand adventures.'

'Sweet child,' he said, kissing me on the forehead.

'Are they true?'

'What say you, child?'

'All your travels and adventures...are they true? Or but mere stories?'

For a moment his face became red and I thought he was going to become angry...but a smile slowly formed across his lips and I relaxed.

'There is so much more, the matters I have witnessed and experienced,' he said, 'that if they were printed, the public would never believe it. Those amazing stories will be told some time in the future, when I al long gone and dead...oh, oh my, my dear, my sweet young thing, look at what you have done to me—*I am hard again!*'

Indeed, he was; and he mounted me and lasted longer the second time.

'I haven't been able to do this in thirty years,' he said, 'long before you were ever born, my dear....'

My skin began to crawl.

When he was done this time, he got dressed and said, 'I hope I might be able to come see you again, C.'

To which I returned: 'I am sure my master will let you.'

INSTALLMENT IX: *In which I meet the famous Detective and his Doctor friend and have a rather curious time with the two nasty gents.*

It was not until three weeks later that Mr. Fogg brought another man to my room for sex—in this case I should say men, since there were two; I had begun to consider that Captain Nemo and Allan Quartermain would be the only ones.

The two men in question were warmly dressed and appeared deathly serious, as if murder and mystery followed and surrounded where their footsteps took their legs and bodies. Mr. Fogg introduced them simply as 'the Detective' and 'the Doctor.'

'For your own protection,' said Mr. Fogg, 'it's best that you do not know their names.'

It didn't matter to me. I didn't have to be told to undress this time; I did so and stood naked in front of their eyes, and their eyes told me they liked what they saw.

The Detective was a tall chap in his late thirties, I'd say, who wore a funny little hat, a cape and smoked a pipe; his companion, the Doctor, was shorter, stouter, and his fifties, I'd say, dressed in stuffy tweed and wearing spectacles. If I were to cross paths with these men on the streets of London, I would most likely believe they were the type that fancied one another the bedchambers…but I knew this was not the case as they were practically drooling over the sight of my naked body.

It was agreed that the Detective would go first. Both the Doctor and Mr. Fogg sat in chairs and observed. The Detective produced a small snuff box and took some white powder out on his finger, placing the finger and powder at his right nostril.

'Must you?' asked the Doctor.

'I must,' said the Detective. He sniffed it all up and smiled. He held out the tiny box to me. 'Care for some, young slut?' he asked me.

I was curious….

'Perhaps not,' said Mr. Fogg, 'not at this moment, sir.'

'You are most likely correct,' said the Detective, and sniffed some more of the stuff. By the glazed look in his eye, I knew that what he ingested was not ordinary snuff. I knew what it was, but did not let on.

The Detective looked nice naked—he may have been slender but his body was all taut muscle. He kept his hat on, which I found funny. He spent his time running his hands up and down and all over my body. 'I so much like how you feel,' he said.

'Good graces, man,' said the Doctor, 'fornicate with her already, will you? Time's a wasting, friend.'

'Right you are,' concurred the Detective, who proceeded to get on top of me, lifting my legs on his shoulders, and doing what men like to do.

Next was the Doctor. He was fat and I did not care for his body at all. His manhood was also fat, and my mouth stretched when I took him that way. Then he had me get on my hands and knees. I was afraid he was going to bugger me but he inserted himself into my…he called it a 'cunny.'

'What a wonderful cunny you have my dear,' he said as he did the old in-out.

What could I say? I said, 'Thank you, sir.'

'So unlike my wife's cunny.'

Mr. Fogg had me next, but this time the Detective and the Doctor stayed to watch. Mr. Fogg seemed to think it was appropriate to bugger me and make a mess on the sheets and my skin.

I cleaned up, and the Detective had me again, and then the Doctor. My body was weak from so many orgasms. I so wanted Mr. Fogg to come to me, but the three men left, not saying a word.

INSTALLMENT X: *In which the Detective comes to see me alone.*

The Detective came to my room the next day. His companion was not with him. Mr. Fogg unlocked the door, allowed the Detective inside, and then closed the door. I found this to be a tad curious and out of the normal mode of operation. The Detective was carrying, in his hand, a violin case.

'Do you play?' I asked.

'I will play for you later,' he responded.

He sat down next to me on the bed. I began to undress and he stopped me, saying, 'Not yet.' He removed, from a pocket, the small box of snuff.

'Perhaps this time you would like to try some,' he said, 'it won't harm you, I promise.'

'I know what it is,' I informed him, 'I am not so innocent, as you may know. It is the product of coca leaves, ground down to fine powder, and has a certain effect on you….'

'A most glorious effect. You have had cocaine before?'

I nodded. I did not tell him, but my uncle had given it to me on a few occasions, during the first few times he made me have sex with him…it made the act more bearable, and even enjoyable.

So I ingested some of the powder through my nostrils and I was on the Detective's level. I must admit I felt very good, no matter how wrong it was to feel good—memories of my uncle's touch and penetrations flooded my mind, but I didn't care. I began to pull the Detective's clothes off him; I touched and kissed his body all over. I said I wanted him inside me. He said, 'I am only interested in oral copulation this time.'

I knew what to do—and it was something I did well: I took the Detective's hard cock into my mouth and swallowed it whole. He shuddered with British delight, saying: 'Oh my!'

After he shot his man seed into my mouth, he returned the favor, which I am not used to by the way: he spread my skinny legs and clamped his mouth on my 'cunny' and brought me to satisfaction twice, whereupon he had me take his manly log, once again stiff, into my gullet.

We sniffed more coca powder and touched each other with greedy, wanton hands. I queried, again, about the violin case. 'Would you like to hear?' he said.

I said I would; perhaps I should have stated otherwise. Nude, the Detective removed the violin, which appeared to be of an antiquarian make; what troubled me (and I am hardly a lass who knows anything about music) is he did not bother to tune it, or rub resin on the bow. I figured he had been playing earlier and did not feel a need to engage in the rudimentary preparations that any common person knew were necessary.

Still, the Detective played, if you could call what he was doing 'playing.' All that came out were screeches and scratches. I resisted the urge to cover my ears and wince.

He stopped.

He looked at me.

He raised a brow.

'So?' he said. 'What do you think?'

'Bravo, sir,' said I.

'Come, now, really.'

'I speak the truth.'

'Then I shall play some more!'

I wish I had it in me to lie. But I was here, for my Master, to please men, not criticize them.

I reached for the snuffbox and indulged myself. I needed to, to endure any more of these sounds! The cocaine helped. The Detective joined me. We kissed and touched and again I took him in my mouth; this time it took him a long while to reach orgasm and he did not return the favor. I did not care. I touched myself between the legs and pleased myself and he pleased himself by 'playing' the violin more.

Then I opened the journal in which I was writing my responses to definitions found in the *Dictionary of the Vulgar Tongue.*[*]

'What do you have there?' asked the Detective.

'Oh something," said I.

'Tell me. Are you a writer?'

'Hardly, sir!'

'But you write!'

'Perhaps I fancy myself something of a poet,' I said.

'And what is your poetry about, if I may ask?'

'It is bad.'

'You mean tripe?'

'I mean of a sexual nature,' I told him, knowing I should have blushed at that moment, but what was there to blush about? His semen was coating my mouth and throat: I was beyond being coy.

---

[*] See the appended document called "A Vulgar Manuscript." –M.H.

He sat next to me and said, 'May I read some? If this is agreeable with you, young C.'

I sighed. I handed him the journal, entitled 'Vulgar' for want of a better cognomen.

The Detective read a few pages, raised his brow, and handed the journal back.

'Interesting,' was his review.

INSTALLMENT XI: *In which my Master brings me a lover I cannot see.*

It was only a week later that Mr. Fogg brought to my room…a man unlike any I had ever laid eyes on, because I never once did see what he looked like.

Mr. Fogg was alone, and I assumed he was there to have his way with me as he did most nights.

I began to undress.

Mr. Fogg did not stop me.

I waited for him to ravish me…I was eager for him to do so, for I was now so used to his attention that I was beginning to depend upon it.

I heard footsteps, and I was aware that someone was standing next to me—I could feel the warm breath of a man, and the eyes of a man, and the heat of a body. But my Master remained by the door.

'Mr. Fogg,' I whispered, 'I fear there is a ghost here!'

My Master laughed, and there was another laugh—so close to me.

I jumped into the bed, pulling the covers over me. 'I know it, Mr. Fogg!' I said. 'Your house must be haunted! There is a ghost among us!'

'No ghost, my sweets,' said a voice from the ether.

'Relax, C.,' said Fogg, taking a few steps closer, 'there is no apparition, but you are quite right: we are not alone. Allow me to introduce one of my more whimsical colleagues, Hawley Griffin. Known in the esoteric circles as He Who Cannot Be Seen, or a Man of the Invisible Realm.'

'I do not understand,' I said.

'Understanding is not required.'

'The girl is scared, poor thing,' said the disembodied voice. 'She should know.'

'She wouldn't understand,' said Fogg.

'Perhaps you underestimate the cunt,' said the voice, which became louder (or closer to me): 'By sheer mistake in my experiments, I entered another dimension. I am here, with you, in your dimension, but at a different angle, thus you cannot see me. But I am here.'

'Oh,' I said.

'You see, she does not understand,' said Fogg.

'But she understands this,' said the voice as the bed sheets began to pull down and reveal my naked body.

I reached for the sheets but Mr. Fogg said, 'Stop! You will let him have you as my other friends have had you. I made a promise for Mr. Griffin's pleasure, and he shall have it.'

Of course, I complied. The sheets continued to be pulled down, and then I felt hands and a mouth all over my body—but there was no body doing this!

Oh, I was frightened, yes, because I still did not understand what was occurring. I looked at Mr. Fogg and his eyes told me everything was all right, as he sat down to watch; I allowed myself to believe my master as I felt the weight of what seemed to be a man get on top of me, as I felt what seemed to be a man's hand spread my legs and what seemed to be a man's penis enter me.

As I was being mysteriously violated, I felt lips at my ears, and I heard endearing and nice words; words that told me to not be scared, to relax; words that told me how beautiful I was and how wonderful I felt.

I relaxed and enjoyed the matter.

When it was over, I felt the weight leave my body; Mr. Fogg stood and left the room, closing and locking the door. I assumed I was alone, again, and after a while I continued to work on the journal called 'Vulgar.'

INSTALLMENT XII: *In which my Master comes and tells me about his other colleagues.*

After some rigorous coitus, his massive tree violating the meat between my legs, Mr. Fogg held me in his mighty arms and said, 'How do you feel about the men I have brought to you? These extraordinary chaps.'

I said, 'If it pleases you, Master.'

'But does it please *you?*'

'All sex does.'

'It pleases me to watch you fuck them,' he said.

'Then that's all that matters, then,' said I.

'I suppose so,' he said; 'I did want to bring over my cohort, Lord Greystoke…he was rather interested in you, but he had to dash off to Africa to aid his wife, Jane. Then I thought of bringing over one of my more dastardly contemporaries, Mr.

Henry Jekyll and his sidekick, Edward Hyde, but I thought better: it would not be a good idea.'

'Why not?'

'Believe me, it would not. You would not be able to handle either of them.'

'Oh.'

'It is true.'

'If you say so.'

'But I may bring others.'

'Bring who you wish, Master.'

'Of them all, whom pleased you the most?'

I did not have to think about it. I said: 'Captain Nemo.'

'But of course.'

* * * * * * *

On the next night together, Mr. Fogg asked me about my 'Vulgar' journal.

'It is coming along,' said I.

'Can I read what you have so far?'

I blushed.

'Or should I wait?' he asked.

'Can you wait, sir?'

'Yes,' he said, 'I am good at waiting.'

INSTALLMENT XIII: *In which Nemo comes to see me again and tells me about the sea.*

Regarding his second visit to me: Captain Nemo did indeed sodomize me quite repeatedly and while I found it uncomfortable at first, I relaxed and enjoyed his ministrations and even begged him to continue to do so, despite the awful mess we made on the bed.

Mr. Fogg grew weary of watching us and left me alone with the sailor.

Between acts of abominable love, Nemo would tell me about his 'submarine' as he called it, and all his adventures upon the high seas, and below such seas as well. His tales were hard to believe, but did I have any reason to doubt him?

'Such well-traveled men lately,' I said in a soft tone, 'why are you all here in London and not out seeking grand experiences that will one day become the matters of books and myth?'

'Because such men need to stop and rest now and then,' said Nemo, 'and male love.'

'Make love?'

'I would like to make love to you,' he said.

'But you have — '

'Up your dirty arse is not making love to a woman.'

'Oh....'

'May I?'

'But of course.'

And so Captain Nemo made slow and tender love to me, and it was very nice.

INSTALLMENT XIV: *In which the Doctor comes to see me, without his companion who cannot play the violin for the life of him!*

It was after Mr. Fogg had his way with me, and I wasn't expecting any more, that the plump, elderly doctor came into my room, softly shutting the door behind him and without my master. I did not bother to cover myself; I was prone, naked, on the bed, Mr. Fogg's seed leaking out between my legs.

'Oh my,' said the Doctor, looking away.

'You were not so bashful before, sir,' said I.

'I am ashamed of how I behaved the last time I was here, you must believe me.'

'I must?'

'Please, dear girl, cover yourself.'

'If you insist, sir,' I said, pulling a sheet around my body.

The Doctor grabbed a chair, pulled it toward the bed, but not too close. He sat down. 'I have come here to ask you a favor, C.,' he said.

I suspected he wanted something perverse and unusual. I sighed and told him that it was my lot to please Mr. Fogg's friends in any manner they deemed necessary.

'It is nothing like that, no!' said the Doctor. 'I am here regarding my friend, you know which friend I speak of….'

'Yes, I do, sir.'

'I am aware that he has come to see you on several occasions.'

'Only one.'

'Yes, well, he intends on coming here again, although I understand your eighty days in Mr. Fogg's captivity are nearing a close.'

'Soon, yes, sir.'

'It is not my place to tell him not to come see you; it is not my place to ask you not to give in to his need for animal lust…but when you leave here, do not go and see him at his place of residence. He will ask, he will beg, he may even bribe you to come see him, but I ask you this now: do not go.'

'Why? If I may query.'

'He has work, important work to do.'

'Such as?'

'Work for Scotland Yard, for Queen and Country. He cannot indulge himself in sexual excess....'

'All men do.'

'He is not like other men.'

'I don't understand why you ask, Doctor. Do you not want him to have me?'

'He must not be distracted.'

'Do you want me all for yourself?'

'Don't be a devil, woman!'

'Oh but I am,' said I, smiling and removing the sheet away from my body. I opened my legs so he could see how swollen my vagina was, how used it was, how it leaked the semen of another man and smelled musty with the act of love.

The Doctor appeared that he wanted to look away, or close his eyes, but the man did neither— for the very fact that he *was* a man. I may have been but a girl, this is true; however, I was quickly learning how men worked, and how I could control them. For the delight of the Doctor's eyes, I touched myself between the legs and moaned.

'What about you, dear Doctor,' said I, 'what of your animal lusts and needs?'

'Indeed, what of them,' the Doctor said as he loosened his collar. 'What the hell, lass, they always get the best of me,' and with that, the fat physician leapt toward the bed and onto me. His mouth was all over my bosom, his spittle on my hard and pink nipples…he even kissed me, which I found repulsive but gave him. His breath stank of the London fog. He removed his pants. He touched me between the legs and flinched. 'You are soiled,' he said.

'My master had me four times in a row,' I told him.

He flipped me over on my belly. 'I shall bugger you then,' he said.

I rolled my eyes and said, 'Do as you wish, sir.'

'It is something my dear wife will never do in bed.'

'Of course, sir,' said I, 'it's what whores like me are for….'

INSTALLMENT XV: *In which the Detective does come to see me.*

We sniffed up a lot of his special snuff and he told me he wanted to do something 'very deviant and awful.'

To which I said, 'Anything, anything, sir....'

He placed a chamber pot in the middle of the room. He had me stand on my knees before it. He stood in front of me, holding his soft manhood in one hand.

'What do you have in mind?' I asked.

'I am going to urinate on you, my dear girl,' he said, 'on your face, in your hair, and even in your mouth. I would like you to drink what I give you, if you can take it.'

'You cannot be serious, sir!' said I in great and wondrous shock at such a suggestion.

'I am very,' he said.

'What ever gave you such an idea?'

'I take it this has never been done to you?'

'No, sir!'

'I saw it be done to prostitutes in a brothel in Germany. Ever since, I have wanted to try it. Will you let me?'

'If you must.'

'Only if you want me to.'

'Proceed as you will.'

What happened next I cannot write about! It's too disgusting and strange…

But oddly pleasurable. So much so that even I am too embarrassed to write anymore!

INSTALLMENT XVI: *In which I have a ghostly visitor.*

It was during my last week of captivity in Mr. Fogg's estate at No. 7 Saville Road that someone, something, came to me in the wee hours of the night. I was sleeping well and dreaming of a grass knoll in Essex when I was awoken to the sensation of a man on top of me and inserting his lobcock into my wet cunny.

I could feel the man, but I could not see him.

'Is it you, Mr. Invisible?' I asked.

A voice at my ear: 'Indeed, young slut, it is I.'

'Does Mr. Fogg know you are here?'

'How astute and aware! No, he does not.'

'Do you fancy yourself an intruder? Do you think you are raping me?'

'I think you would like that.'

'Oh but I do,' I told the ghost, 'I do....'

'Tell me then.'
'Rape me.'
'Tell me like you mean it!'
'Rape me good, sir!'

INSTALLMENT XVII: *In which my Master's manservant spanks me good.*

Passepartout came to me like he did often, usually after Mr. Fogg had his way. This night, there was no sign of my keeper.

'He's at the Reform Club,' said Passepartout, 'all night, I assume.'

'A game of cards?' I inquired.

'Most likely,' said Passepartout, 'it's always a matter of wager with our master.'

'I wonder what he will win this time,' I mused; 'perhaps another young woman to keep in this room after I leave?'

'No man can be that lucky trice! Not even Phileas Fogg!'

'Trice?'

'There was one other before you.'

'A captive girl?'

'A lady…ten years your senior.'

'When?'

'Oh…a little over a year ago, I believe.'

'Who was she?'

'Someone….'

'Who?'

'I dare not say!'

'Why? Passepartout, why?'

'For one, she was married….'

'A married woman! How did she…?'

'The same as you, I fear.'

'She was won in a card game?'

Passepartout nodded, and looked as if he was about to weep.

'Why so sad?' I asked.

'She was a fine, tender woman who fell prey to her husband's awful mind and bad luck at cards,' said Passepartout as he sat next to me on the bed.

'Oh,' is all I could say, and I wondered what she had to endure while she was confined to this very room and bed. I became excited by these thoughts, so I reached between Passepartout's legs and tried to stimulate the little Frenchman.

'I will miss you, C.'

'Why?'

'I have become fond of you.'

'Of a whore?'

'Why not?'

'You like me then?'

'Very much so.'

'Then show me.'

He did. And after, he asked to read my 'Vulgar' journal. I said he could. He took his time sifting through the sixty odd pages. 'This is wonderful poetry!' he exclaimed, slapping me on the behind.

I laughed. 'You jest.'

"I do not!'

'It is hardly poetry.'

'It looks like poetry; it reads as such.'

'It is dog real,' I told him, 'mere gibberish, full of nasty words and imagery.'

'Oh but I like it.'

'I am happy that you do.'

'What made you…?'

'This,' I said, handing him the copy of *The Dictionary of the Vulgar Tongue*. 'Our master gave it to me.'

'He is always the one to corrupt minds with all his notions, is he not?' queried Passepartout.

'So it would seem,' I returned.

'Or maybe it is the other way around,' mused the little Frenchman.

I gave him a curious glance.

'Perhaps you, and all women such as your-self, are the true impetus behind the secret sexual desires of great men.'

To that, I laughed loudly.

'You a terrible, awful young woman!' he exclaimed.

'Am I now?'

'*Oui.* You know you are!'

'Perhaps this is true. Perhaps,' I chortled, just to annoy the silly chap.

'You should be punished,' said he, 'you should be spanked, mademoiselle.'

'I agree.'

'I shall bend you over my knee.'

'Do it, if you must!'

And he did.

'I shall spank you,' he said.

'I deserve every whack,' said I.

'I will show no mercy.'

'I would not expect otherwise, you dirty frog.'

'What did you say?'

'FROG!'

Whack.

Well, he spanked me good. He left my buttocks quite black and blue.

'Do you want more?' he kept asking.

I was in tears as I said, 'Give me what you have. Is your hand not tired by now?'

'My hand throbs,' he said, 'but I will give you more, if that's what you require.'

'I require a lot, sir,' I told him.

'Then you shall receive....'

And did.

And that was the last I saw of M. Passepartout. To be frank, I could live a full and happy life if I never encountered him again. He was an agreeable fellow, but I have never been very partial to the French.

INSTALLMENT XVIII: *In which I have my final night with Mr. Phileas Fogg.*

'Tomorrow you are free,' said my Master, 'tomorrow you can walk away from this bed, this room, and me.'

'And what if I do not want to?' asked I. 'What if I prefer what I have here, to what waits for me in the outside world?'

'Do you actually enjoy what I have put you through?'

'Do you need to ask?'

He smiled. 'Oh you little wench, give me a kiss.'

I kissed Mr. Fogg and I said, 'I can stay.'

'You cannot. Your uncle would be furious. I would not be honoring the gentlemen's agreement we had. It was eighty days, and then I return you to him.'

'I am twenty now, I will not go back to my uncle. Even if my contract with him still has five years on it."

'When did you turn twenty…?'

'A few weeks ago.'

'And you said nothing?'

'Was I required to?'

'I would have brought you a birthday cake!'

'I do not care for cake.'

'I would have….'

'Hush, my Master,' I said, touching his fine bearded face.

'Tonight is our last night together, it should be special and nice,' he said.

'And so it shall. What would you like me to do?'

'I find that I shall miss you.'

'Then I can stay.'

'You cannot.'

'Did you find yourself missing the other woman who was in my place? The woman who was another man's wife that you had won in a game?'

Mr. Fogg's expression changed. He asked, 'How did you know…?'

I acted coy.

'That damned Passepartout!'

'It is not his fault,' I said, "I pried the information out of him.'

'With your mouth no doubt!'

I acted coy.

'Oh you wonderful trollop!' he said, and began to tickle me.

'Stop!' I yelled, and he stopped. Then I asked: 'So did you, sir?'

'Did I?'

'Miss your married woman sex slave?'

'In a fashion.'

'And me?'

'Very much so.'

'I can and will stay and be your lover and maybe even your wife,' I suggested.

'That could never be possible,' he said. 'Your uncle.'

'To blazes with my uncle!'

'There are rules of engagement we live by, at the Reform Club.'

'God forbid I should interfere with that.'

'Do not bring God into this, lass,' said he, 'this is no place for the Deity.'

Mr. Fogg made love to me, and after the lovely act, I said, 'I will not go back to my uncle. Ever.'

'That is your decision, C. My obligation is merely to set you free from this room and my home. What you do after that is beyond my control, and his, I should say. But you need to know that your uncle, Mr. Henry, will be here at nine a.m. sharp to retrieve you.'

'Then I shall leave at seven!'

'Yes, perhaps you should. I can give you some money, to help you leave….'

'That will not be necessary,' I said, 'for I have plans.'

'Plans?'

'If you can have a carriage ready for me at seven a.m. sharp, I will be heading to the docks….'

'The docks?'

'Where Captain Nemo's ship, the *Nautilus* is waiting. Where,' I said proudly, 'Nemo himself is waiting for me.'

'Why you crafty whore,' said Fogg.

I smiled, not so coyly.

'You made plans!'

'Indeed,' I said, 'the Captain wishes to show me a bit of the world.'

'He has a wife and children back home, you know.'

I knew. 'Does it matter?' said I. 'He will return me to London, if I wish, when our journey together is over.'

'Should you come back to London, do look me up,' he said.

'I plan to, sir.'

'I will show you the parts of the world that Nemo does not.'

'I would like that.'

'And maybe your uncle's anger will diminish by then.'

'I do not care about him. He was terrible to me, just terrible.'

'And I?'

'Always wonderful.'

'I must have you many times tonight,' he said.

'Just so I'm not too weary to leave and go to sea in the morning,' I said.

'Never,' he said.

And when he made love to me, I climaxed and explained, 'Oh, Mr. Fogg, yes, Mr. Fogg, you do that so good, Mr. Fogg!'

'Call me by my first name,' he muttered into my ear.

'Oh, Phileas, my *Phileas*,' I bemoaned in pure delight, *'fuck me hard, you Byronic bastard!'*

A VULGAR MANUSCRIPT

as composed by "C"
while in the captive hands of
Phileas Fogg[*]

---

[*] These pages were found loose and bound by a rusty clip in the back of C's journal. There was no indication of a proposed order, so I took the liberty of alphabetizing them. The use of ampersands and short hand are as written by C, not editorially imposed. –R.R.

VULGAR: 1. characterized by ignorance of or lack of good breeding or taste: *vulgar ostentation.* 2. indecent; obscene, lewd: *a vulgar work; a vulgar gesture.* 3. crude; coarse; unrefined: *a vulgar peasant.* 4. of, pertaining to, or constituting the vulgar ordinary people in a society: *the vulgar masses.* 5. current; popular; common: *vulgar idols; a vulgar success; vulgar beliefs.* 6. spoken by, or being in the language spoken by, the people generally; vernacular: *a vulgar translation of the Greek text of the New Testament.* 7. lacking in distinction, aesthetic value, or charm; banal; ordinary: *a vulgar painting; vulgar architecture.* 8. *Archaic.* the common people. 9. *Obs.* the vernacular.

The vulgar tongue
found its way in
among the common rabble
& I came with them & came along.
This is the vulgate:
a holy book of holy words—
coarse, crude, unrefined
& mine.

ARBOR VITAE. A man's penis.

A tree & a valley: the landscape is corrugated after all,
like something steel but sweaty
hiding in our small clothes;
our bodies supersede us,
your saliva a drizzle—it stirs me,
my mouth a sinkhole
hinged with a jaw.

ATHANASIAN WENCH or QUINCUNQUE VULT. A forward girl, ready to oblige every man that shall ask her.

I put the first foot forward
& found myself
obliged to dance
with a gdansk man,
his reference vague. Still,
there was something
worth the going in for.
I was yet a tender lass,
a girl of twenty-three,
but the bacon fed boys
with their greasy smiles
had found me long ago.
I haven't broke my ankle yet,
but my club foot drags a bit.

BITCH. A she dog or doggess; the most offensive appellation that can be given to an English woman, even more provoking that that of whore, as may be gathered from the regular Billingsgate or St. Giles's answer—"I may be a whore, but can't be a bitch."

Every time I hear my name I think of you who named me,
so that I may be a whore, but can't be a bitch.
I've got an itch up my arse so why don't you come & bite it
& stop sniffing around the bush.
Gods & dogs make doggesses & goddesses & all
these esses are slithering around your toes with the repeated
esse sum ergo I am.
I am that I am is how you'll believe me
said the burning bush to the burning man
& I am
a whore, a bitch, an apple-biter, a snake-pit
in love with a lovely git,
& I am by whatever name you call me.

TO BLOW THE GROUNSILS. To lie with a woman on the floor.

The linoleum is cold this morning
& only your cock is slippered,
the tap water is running
& the tea pot is blowing
& you roll by like a train
& get up and butter the toast.

A BLOWSE, or BLOWSABELLA. A woman whose hair is dishevelled, and hanging about her face; a slattern.

My hair hangs in slats about my face
that you grab with baby fists & twist,
pulling the blinds closed
so the neighbors won't see
that you like me.

CARVEL'S RING. The private parts of a woman. Ham Carvel, a jealous old doctor, being in bed with his wife, dreamed that the Devil gave him a ring, which, so long as he had it on his finger, would prevent his being made a cuckold: waking he found he had got his finger the Lord knows where. See Rabelais, and Prior's versification of the story.

My antlered man, a hart
chasing hind, you're always behind
thinking you've found my heart;
you've only found a ring
to wear for an hour or two,
worth less than the cheap bit of metal you placed around my finger
that turned said finger green.
The devil's right you know:
you'll never get a hold
of me except with your finger of flesh.
Lord knows I tried to tell you
I am what I am
and it's you that have made it so because you
named it so.

COCK ALLEY or COCK LANE. The private parts of a woman.

Who would have thought that I had so many names
so many entryways,
but the stopsigns and the streetlights these days
make it rough going
and that's for cock-sure,
but you know my name & you know the way
& you'll find a way whether it be broadway or main,
or a dark alley beside the trolley tracks that no one knows
but you & some dark part or place
that is me.

CUNT. The χοννος of the Greek, and the *cunnus* of the Latin dictionaries; a nasty name for a nasty thing: *un con Miege*.

What you touch with your lips
I want you
to say with your tongue:
the same,
every nasty thought you had
inside your nasty head
is voiced in me—
Cunt.
Vox, a box of light that says my name.

DELLS. Young buxom wenches, ripe and prone to venery, but who have not lost their virginity, which the *upright man* claims by virtue of his prerogative; after which they become free for any of the fraternity. Also a common strumpet.

In the valleys & in the dells
a fraternity of beasts gives chase
as is their wont. The landscape calls
for it & echoes the game,
played so quietly before.
Calling my name,
parting parched lips with tongues,
the sound was heard
throughout the land,
and it was said
kingdom come, thy will be done, on earth
as it is in heaven.
So it was, I twisted my ankle, and gave birth
to a new name,
the christening heard
from the lowlands to the hills
where the trumpets blasted song,
declaring, with great obsequiousness,
as the banner rolled out & my name was pronounced
in the vulgar tongue—*strumpet*.
You parted my lips with the word,
now heard in the lowlands, in the valleys,

upon the frosted peaks of mountaintops.
Our delivery into vulgarity, as sheep
flocked around our manger
bright with the light
of glowing, white, sweaty skin,
was the salvation of the dry and cracking carcasses
of all the herded beats.

DILDO. [From the Italian *diletto*, q. d. a woman's delight; or from our word *dally*, q. d. a thing to play withal.] Penis-succedaneus, called in Lombardy Passo Tempo. *Bailey*.

I pass the time & it passes by,
it is my delight, to have you by my side, a forever
thing well formed by plastic & by mold,
more constant in its attentions
& silent than the mouthy heads
of blooded men.
It speaks to a mouth known but little,
except by name & reputation.

DIRTY PUZZLE. A Nasty slut.

A weave of words interlocked on grimy newspaper print
that dirties my hands, lily white.
There are never enough names
to call you,
my love; I have taken to searching
for clues
in the papers,
for signs
on the streets,
for dirty words
of the conjuring sort,
locked in a grid of other words;
you are somewhere in between
2 across and 33 down,
a papal bequest & an Oscar winner.

TO DOCK. To lie with a woman. The cull docked the dell all the darkmans; the fellow laid with the wench all night. Docked smack smooth; one who has suffered an amputation of his penis from a venereal complaint. He must go into dock; s sea phrase, signifying that the spoken of must undergo a salivation. Docking is also a punishment inflicted by sailors on the prostitutes who have infected them with the venereal disease; it consists in cutting of their clothes, petticoats, shift and all, close to their stays, and then turning them into the street.

You docked in my dell all the darkmans long.
You hovered above & then came down below.
You cut off my clothes & then shift & all
turned me into the street,
not knowing, what I already was,
the street, the common
whore, vulgar & stronger than you,
naked & shining bright with sweat & semen of yours.

EVE'S CUSTOM-HOUSE, where Adam made his first entry. The monosyllable.

I was custom made for you my dear
by our lord and savior,
(dearly departed for shinier places)
out of clay & dirt
& mud & muck,
I've run out of luck,
but I'm still a good fuck, my love,
come down in the mud with me,
& pay your toll to the man,
your own vulgar soul.
Why not; they sell it in a can
these days.

FLAT COCK. A female.

The flat of your cock lies against my thigh: pretty slumber,
having surrendered to me, ready for more,
a good little whore,
you recognized me, the same girl as before,
your nemesis, a hole to bury yourself in,
you wouldn't even have to dig.
The floorboards of the coffin are rotten with worms
with teeth that eat through satin.

FRUITFUL VINE. A woman's private parts, i.e. that has *flowers* every month, and bears fruit in nine months.

My great tap root is wriggling,
embroiled in the toil of dirt,
tickling the nightcrawlers in dense soil,
curling its aperture around the vulgar presence of the land.
There was nothing immaculate in this conception
that conceived of me & has me bleed for it.
Cow shit fertilizes the soil & a farmer's cock pecks at seeds.
The veiny vines in his chicken limbs warble
up through his throat as he announces the day
and the end of me.

GAYING INSTRUMENT. The penis.

All you gay young lads & dandies too
are made so glad & come to such good use,
dancing on whore-house bed sheets,
dawdling with the bell-dames until the church bell rings &
you tuck your shirts in & tuck the rest away
& sing a merry hymn to jesus from your little pew,
eyeing the pastor's cod-piece, as the bottom of his robes dance
like a bell upon the dusty floorboards. A hymnal comes
to good use and a lapidary smiles at the engraving on the tomb.

GINGAMBOBS. Toys, bawbles; also a man's privities. See Thingambobs.

Up in the garret there are all sorts of treasures & trinkets.
It is dark here & everyone has their trousers down.
The steps grunt & groan as you ascend
& the door knob has a tricky catch,
but just when you have lost your breath,
the door opens out on you & the gingambobs run loose,
wild monkeys trapped for years,
their eyes atrophied from lack of use.

**HAT. Old Hat; a woman's privities: because fre-
quently felt.**

All the bald-pated men these days wear caps
& there is sense in that
for who would want to catch a cold.
Grandmothers too wear ones with a pretty sash
& their dogs sit upon them
to warm their laps
& in my lap too; gentleman come seeking hats,
asking after the possibility of haberdashery,
& how could I send such gentleman away
on such cold winter days.
As a matter of course, I never do.
Come one, come all!
One size fits most & is frequently felt
to be most fitting & very suitable,
being as it were.

HORN COLIC. A temporary priapism.

My baby cries at me at night & lays
his head upon my lap.
This gives way to quite a different sort of affair,
he calls me lady, he calls me mum, he calls me whore, he calls me
fuck
and I say yes, yes, yes,
I say leave the work to me.
I am as you've named me,
a girl with dirty work to do.

HUSSY. An abbreviation of housewife, but now always used as a term of reproach; as, How now, hussy? or, She is a light hussy.

Without house or wifeliness I came
to hussiness & I don't how it all came to be,
only now it is. You know a hussy
when you see one, don't you
see me, one big, fat hussy down
on her knobby knees
praying her lusty, hussy prayers.
Hussy angels attend me & salivate
over my salvation,
& so does Stan,
the hairy man
from down the street
who gives me the time of day
nowadays.

IMPURE. A modern term for a lady of easy virtue.

What is left for purity in modernity
when there is nothing left of originality
only miles & miles of duplicity—
the paperwork's astounding,
our letter-sized jaws spitting out
cottage cheese curds of words,
that have come before—
everything a duplication, a lazy fabrication
of the original sin—
the original fuck—
an Adam & an Eve,
a grunt & a groan,
a thrust & a moan.
Virtue is easy these days—
if you wear the right hat
& don't let yourself run to fat
you can be pure as the next girl
in a white dress
mouthing words at an altar.

JIG. A trick. A pleasant jig; a witty arch trick. Also a lock or door. The feather-bed jig; copulation.

A jig & a jog & a hippety hop,
we do the two-step & the charleston too,
modern dance stylings & it all comes down to this.
A man a woman a jig.
A distraction, a trick
my cunt & your dick.
Why go to the nightclub at all with my fat ass and my leather pants,
your forty dollar cologne and freshly shaved blade of bone.
I've got a hatch of bone too,
along my hip,
it's a short trip to my house
& I'm home alone,
the door is open
& I've left the dog a bone.

KNOCK. To knock a woman; to have carnal knowledge of her. To knock off; to conclude, phrase borrowed from the blacksmith. To knock under; to submit.

They never have the courtesy to ring the bell,
always knocking at my door, saying this
is what I asked for. & the habit of them
knocks around my head so I can't knock it loose.
They don't know my name, but they know me commonly
cuz my skirt is short & my blouse is low
& I show what it is I am—
fat gams, a lazy eye, a few pounds of flesh
at hip & thigh, & breast;
they don't know themselves as well as this
covered under careful layers of underwear
& outerwear; they haven't stood naked
in front of the mirror without a leaf of lettuce, a cape
of cloth that belies the flesh away from vulgarity.

LADYBIRDS. Light or lewd women.

I wear my shame like a feather boa.
It tickles
my ears &
it tickles
your fancy.
The balls
of your feet
are ticklish too & your tickle tail
is not a prick for ticklish women.
Red lips, pink cheeks,
I know when it's best not to laugh.
I fly south for a reason.

**LOBCOCK. A large relaxed penis: also a dull inani-
mate fellow.**

Oh, homunculus I hear the dim-witted dice rattling in your head.
Not to belittle you—you are, after all, a fabulous little fellow,
a lobcock, no cock & bull, a smaller version of the larger thing,
my little plaything, my dolly do, I've had a crush on you
& only now can admit it. It's a small wonder,
I'll never leave you,
please don't forsake
your name,
I love the shame
I feel
when I'm with you.

MADGE. The private parts of a woman.

Madge, a diminutive of Margaret.
Little Margaret, little girl,
makes her way through the world.
Her cunt leads the way,
a badge she wears,
to prove she's a woman.
The men know her as Madge,
and rarely as Margaret,
for she is not a rare girl,
but common as they come,
a madge among many,
but they do not love her less
for all that, for who would want
a Margaret when they could have a Madge instead?
Her name is engraved
on the walls
of truck stops urinals,
on the lips
of men who want
a name dirty enough
to match the drive
of their desire.

MERKIN. Counterfeit hair for women's privy parts

I had a well-combed goatee on my lower lip,
a merkin bit to match the hair on your hairlip.
In the back seat, you saw I wasn't for real, only a mawkish girl
who wasn't yet coarse enough for you.
You thought better of me,
but these mustached mouths are all the same,
facing up or facing down,
& you've had it everyway,
but I was your first
counterfeit that fit so well—& every afterwards,
common enough for you
& you didn't think much on me

MONOSYLLABLE. A woman's commodity.

I've got it dressed in gold lame
cuz it's worth its weight in gold.
One word, one roll of the tongue, one single thing heard,
it's all you can think of & it beats against your head
like a battering ram
cunt cunt cunt cunt
fuck fuck fuck fuck
let me in let me in let me in.
A shield of vulgar names,
can't arrest it,
it's just an answer to your knock,
one word unheard, whichever you like.
It takes cash credit or check by the hour.

NEB, or NIB. The bill of a bird, and the slit of a pen. Figuratively, the face and mouth of a woman; as She holds up her neb; she hold her mouth up to be kissed.

The neb of my mouth, the slit of a pen that scribbles words unheard against your neck.
You've got words for me & I've got some for you;
I hold my mouth up,
take it & shut it with your own
before we speak unneeded things.
It can be dark & quiet in that cavern we call a mouth.

NUB. The neck; also coition.

Here's the thing,
the rub of the nub.
rub a dub dub,
it's three to a tub,
you me & nub.
The bikinis & the trunks come off
and we're nubs of flesh
caught on a hump.

**OCCUPY. To occupy a woman; to have carnal knowl-
edge of her.**

Colonel, the charnel house is occupied.
There's sweating, fucking corpses in here
trying to get to know each other.
Something simply must be done
to put an end to this madness.
Hamcocks are copulating with beefsteaks &
fresh meat is brought in from the trenches hourly.
There are no vacancies, Colonel, the muttonchops
are not love incarnate.

ONE OF US, or ONE OF MY COUSINS. A woman of the town, a harlot.

She is a willful brazen beast, she is one of us.
Take her home & clean her up, wipe the paint
off her brow,
she'll always be one of us.
The less she's got on
the more you'll see
her resemblance to you & me.
The large strips of skin that sweat for want
of air, enclosed in a letterbox of names
rolling credits across the screen.

PIECE. A wench. A damned good or bad piece; a girl who is more or less active and skilful in the amorous congress. Hence the (*Cambridge*) toast, May we never have a *piece* (peace) that will injure the constitution.

You've got me piece meal,
a chunk of flesh & guts at a time,
& under the skin
burns the original sin
untapped by you;
your reach is shallow & lacks imagination.
You only have two hands
to hold names for me.

PUBLIC LEDGER. A prostitute: because, like that paper, she is open to all parties.

To think you could open me
& read me simply
by opening my thighs.
Because you've touched my vulgar skin
doesn't mean you've yet kissed a vulgar thought
in my head. Twenty bucks gets you in
but doesn't tell you which way to go.
My skin is a palimpsest
of other touches,
other fingers
having left their print
on me.
Can you read
what it is to be me
& be touched by you
who thinks you're touching
skin,
not the writing
tablet of men who've all said
different things the same way?
Can you read
the traces
of others?

QUAIL-PIPE. A woman's tongue; also a device to take birds of that name by imitating their call. Quail-pipe boots; boots resembling a quail-pipe, from the number of plaits; they were much worn in the reign of Charles II.

My tongue imitates your call by naming itself.
Your tongue is thick & the words stumble out.
You gag on a mumble, tendering change at me
because you don't have a dollar to your name.
Our kiss is awkward, like hungry starlings in their fetal nest.
We can't quite find what will satisfy,
eyes glued shut with flesh,
mouths larger than our souls.

ROMP. A forward, wanton girl, a tomrig. Grey, in his notes to Shakespeare, derives it from arompo, and animal found in South Guinea, that is a man eater.

Things go a different way in South Guinea,
even the cigarettes are sweeter there.
The men let the girls take a turn
pulverizing things with their mandibles,
spitting things out in salivated chunks called words
that are dull with use and digestion.
We're all hoydens in short skirts with lazy eyes
& breasts that look both ways before crossing.
The environment is conducive there,
the indigenous repopulate in a jiffy.

RUTTING. Copulating. Rutting time; the season when deer go to rut.

The population is copulating
behind closed doors & drawn shades;
even the palmetto bugs are flying around the house
in a frenzy of tropical heat.
We're all stuck in a rut
fucking our guts out
as the ice melts in the back of the pick-up
& the maggots are breeding in the store-bought steak
cuz 'tis the season
when merry men are made
and flies circle round sweaty heaving bodies
like small vultures.

SCREW. To copulate. A female screw; a common prostitute. to screw one up; to exact upon one in a bargain or reckoning.

The house I've built has one door.
I've screwed it shut tight
& you're stuck in this shack with me.
There's nothing left to do,
here,
left to our devices,
at last ignorant,
the day shut out with rusty blinds & hotel drapes,
we sleep as babies sucking thumbs.

SLATTERN. A woman sluttishly negligent in her dress.

Tonight, my love, I haven't dressed at all;
I haven't even painted
my lashes, my love, I'm in my original skin.
I'm a sack of organs beating in your direction,
so use me at your own discretion,
my negligence has been
deliberate.

TROLLOP. A lusty coarse sluttish woman.

The city is far off & there are no cabs
in this part of Hoboken.
It's hard to be a trollop this time of year.
The old men keep to their space
heaters in rent-controlled boxes.
The gerrymander's been set & I've been drawn in
with the rest of the whores
who live as the street
would have them with dirt
upon their ankles & runs in their stockings.
Skyrises like candles raised
against the night toss their light
down on me,
in the street;
they've lost their sense
of bodies with feet
on the ground,
of mud & muck,
their windows being washed by men dangling on slats of fear;
they've lost their pound of flesh
and forgotten gravity,
the thighs of their occupants being erased by health club machines;
they've lost their mind
of what is low,
their penthouses being filled with air so thin
& it's lonely down below
& low is

the way I go,
following the slope of the ground
all the way back downtown.

TRUMPERY. An old whore, or goods of no value; rubbish.

The wastebuckets are over-
flowing with reams of paper & empty boxes,
cans milked dry. In this land
called Trumpery we wear trash—
bags like fur-lined mantles. There are torches
& voices echoing through alleys
saying things never heard, words
tossed out with the trash, words
your mother washed your mouth out with soap for, words
I've packrat-ed away
for the day
when they'll come looking
for something to say.

UNFORTUNATE WOMAN. Prostitutes: so termed by the virtuous and compassionate of their own sex.

My sex is mine own, not yours—
you can't be a woman,
you don't smoke the same sticks as me.
I smoke unfiltered
and true as tar.
You smoke mentholated
like a chipmunk,
nuts in cheeks,
trying to look delicate
with a stick of nicotine
poised between the furrows
of a fur-lined paw.
I suck in, I blow out, I get the job done,
the game's the same
& has nothing to do
with fortune.

TO VAMP. To pawn anything. I'll vamp it, and tip you the cole: I'll pawn it and give you the money. Also to refit, new dress, or rub up old hats, shoes or other wearing apparel; likewise to put new feet to old boots. Applied more particularly to the quack bookseller.

Rub up against this old hat, johnny blue,
I've vamped up my tits tonight just for you,
they're rouged to the hilt
& ready to knock
against you, so sail on in
to this dock,
all the pilings
have been plucked clean of barnacles

VELVET. To tip the velvet; to put one's tongue into a woman's mouth. To be upon the velvet; to have the best of a bet or match. To the little gentleman in velvet; i.e. the mole that threw up the hill that caused Crop (King William's horse) to stumble; a toast frequently drank by Tories and Catholics in Ireland.

Red velvet, red carpet,
that down my windpipe rolls
to all the games below. Come on in,
it's soft as saliva,
as skin.
You can catch a glimpse
of my red, red heart
thumping on its beat
somewhere far below.

WAGTAIL. A Lewd woman.

I shake my tail,
it's an impetus of bone.
My lycra-bottomed cheeks play
their own game.
The sway and swag
of skin over bone,
inevitable as gravity,
your fall
into my bed.

WAP. To copulate, to beat. If she won't wap for a winne, let her trine for a make; if she won't lie with a man for a penny, let her hand for a halfpenny. Mort wap-apace; a woman of experience, or very expert at the sport.

Mort wap-apace with black lace,
the thick lashes and all the trappings of the game.
My intentions are vulgar,
my motives are coarse
like the black wires on my head,
not a thing of finery,
but of blood and veins
and guts and brains.
Can you catch my pace?

WHIRLYGIGS. Testicles.

Whirly gig, let's dance a jig,
be careful of the gears and cogs
they'll snap your fingers off.
The machine never shuts down,
not even for easter.
There is a beast turning
the rusty crankshaft
in the back
is what they say.
He's hairy and he's got us by the guts.

WHOREPIPE. The penis.

It's time to pay the piper, so to speak.
It's been a good long week since you've been this way,
and I know a little game we could play,
so let's open up the drywall and expose
the plumbing in this place.
We'll have to get our hands
a little dirty for the proper fix.

XANTIPPE. The name of Socrates's wife: now used to signify a shrew or scolding wife.

Her lips never shut,
Always open on a bitch,
I'd shut them with my mouth,
if I thought I could,
but it'd do no good,
her vulgar tongue simply
seeks to find its way
inside my head,
up into my brain
and I let it.
All the words she's said
and more
had been there long before
stewing around in a cesspool
you call philosophy,
but I all really want
are the red red lips
of Xantippe,
without the eroding drip
of words.
I was glad to drink the hemlock.
It tasted sweet
as her lips.

YELLOW. To look yellow; to be jealous. 'I happened to call on Mr. Green, who was out: on coming home, and finding me with his wife, he began to look confounded and blue, as was, I thought, a little yellow.'

The bile's rising
in my throat,
it makes me want
to choke,
when I see you
in your underwear,
with hip exposed,
thinking of another man
in that soft brain
of yours.
It's your body
that's hard.
I elide against it
and omit the sin between us
but slide off;
you're slick as marble.
Does he pet you like an eel?
Does he pet your pelted unshaved skin?
Does he pelt your brain like rain,
the shape of your thoughts supplied by him?
The slope of your thigh reshaped by him,
the cells sloughed off to reveal
new skin.

APPENDIX

The Strange Case of C.'s Return

by J. W.

To my friend _____ _____, the usually impeccable amateur detective of many of my written accounts, C. was quite the woman, the woman he was enamored with for a time; she wasn't *the woman* as was Irene Adler (see "A Scandal in Bohemia"), and in the case of C., as with Ms. Adler, I say of my friend: "as a lover he would have placed himself in a false position."

As for myself, I was ashamed of what I had done with C. while she was the sexual slave of Phileas Fogg. I am a married man, after all; but like all men, blissfully wedded or not, I had my weakness, and a woman such as C. found herself quite in her skin when exploiting such weaknesses—for example, my friend the amateur detective.

I had called upon him one day, a cold autumn day, and found him deep in the act of oral copulation with C. That is, she had him deep in her mouth, from what I could tell, lying in front of him, her body between his legs.

'My dear fellow,' said my friend, smiling and taking a whiff from the contents of his snuff box, 'life is infinitely stranger than anything which the mind of man could invent.'

'For the love of—what are you doing, man?' I exclaimed, but admittedly, I was not in as much shock as I may have appeared.

The woman, C., removed my friend's penis from her mouth, looked at me, winked, and said, 'Why, hello, Doctor."

'Ma'am,' I nodded.

She went back to her wet-sounding ministrations.

'You can have her next, if that's what you care for,' said my friend.

'I assure you, it is not!'

'Your eyes tell me other wise, my dear old friend, and C. here has told me how you came to visit her alone, when she was up at Phileas' abode.'

'I had heard she left London!'

'Yes, there was quite a row with her uncle and Phileas, or so I have heard.'

'I heard she left the country.'

'She did, with Nemo no less. That was what? Four months ago? And now she is back, and now she is here, and now I am about to spend myself in her delicious little mouth,' to which my friend did, his back stiff, his mouth agape, as he reached that ver-reachable moment all men crave.

I shuddered, just watching. Why do you ask? Because, damn it all, I wanted to be my friend at that moment; I wanted C.'s mouth on my prick! This chance could have come, I suppose, had not we been interrupted by that hodgepodge of wayward, unwashed misfits that my friend often used to help in the details of his cases.

They rushed up the stairs and into the room, all half dozen of them, smelling of mischief and the back alleys of Whitechapel. When they saw C., knelt in the lap of their hero, the boys stopped and stared and whistled.

'Ah here they are!' said my friend.

'And who be these young hooligans?' asked C., standing on her feet.

The boys again whistled.

'Why, they are the Baker Street Irregulars!' my friend said with glee. 'And I have invited them all here to sample you, my dear!'

'Hip hip hooray!' cried the boys.

'Do you mean all of them?' asked C.

'Of course,' said my friend.

'Why, that could very well be quite fun,' said C.

'Naturally,' said my friend, 'undoubtedly.'

'Hey, love,' said one of the boys, 'show us whatcha looks like underneath them knickers, eh?'

C. looked at my detective friend.

The detective raised a brow and said, 'Not a bad suggestion. Show these boys what you have to offer, C.'

C. took her time removing her outer and under garments. The boys became very anxious, as did I.

'Hurry up now!' said the boys. 'Let's get on with the show!'

I silently agreed.

Finally, the whore was as bare as the days she was born…which I gather wasn't too long ago.

The Baker Street boys were drooling like a pack of vicious wolf cubs.

'Oh such young men!' sighed C. 'Who shall I suck first?'

'Do you think you can take them all on, my sweet?' asked the detective.

'Oh,' she said, 'I believe I can.'

And so she did. For the next hour and a half, I watched in utter disgust and fascination as C. took on one boy after the other. First, she took each in her mouth until they spent themselves, and like boys often do, that didn't take long; then she fornicated with each boy, starting one at a time and then two (one in her mouth, one on the other end) and finally three as she opened her derriere for whatever lad which to go that route.

'Such beasts!' I said to my friend.

'Such fine and happy creatures, are they not?' returned my friend.

'But why?'

'I owe them, and now they will owe me even more.'

'Indeed.'

When they were done with her, C. was quite the mess, lying on the floor, covered in semen and urine. 'Scatter yourselves to the wind now,' I said to them. They laughed and whistled as they made their way down the street and back to the streets.

It was my turn. I hovered above the girl, pulling out my swollen penis. 'There are terrible things I wish to do to you,' I said.

'I know,' she said, 'but wait!' She quickly stood up and fetched her handbag. 'I almost forgot, in all this excitement…. I have a letter I was to deliver to Mr. ___. For his eyes only.' She removed a wrinkled letter with my friend's name on it. 'Here you go,' she said and handed over the letter.

My friend eyed the communiqué with amusement at first, and then apprehension; there was something about the handwriting that he recognized. Abruptly, he tore open the letter and read.

His face flushed, and then he looked at C. with ter-ror in his eyes.

'Where and when were you given this?' he asked her.

'In Italy, when Captain Nemo came to port in Venice,' she replied.

'By courier?'

'No.'

'By…?'

'The kind gentleman who penned the letter, I presume,' she said, 'he told me he was an old friend of yours.'

'Good Lord,' said the Detective.

'Sir?'

'Did you…did you have sexual relations with the man?'

'But of course,' she said with a smile, wiping away some of the boy's semen from her face.

'Good Lord, no,' said my friend.

'What is it?'

I coughed. My friend looked at me as if I had just walked into the room. He handed over the let-ter for me to read. It was short, but to the point. It read:

We really do tread the same ground, my esteemed nemesis, now that I have violated this young tender morsel that I know you are fond of.

—M.

'Oh no,' said I with a deep sigh.

'What is it?' asked C.

My friend began to weep.

'I don't understand,' the girl exclaimed. 'I simply do not understand!' she cried.

'No, my dear,' retorted I, walking away from the pathetic sight, 'you do not.'

www.ingramcontent.com/pod-product-compliance
Lightning Source LLC
Chambersburg PA
CBHW020651180626
46816CB00003B/1225